Darkness 101

lessons were
learned

EDITED BY

Jonathan Reddoch
Elizabeth Suggs

FREE GIFT

Thank you for your purchase. To claim your free e-book please visit www.CTPFiction.com

DARKNESS 101:
Lessons Were Learned

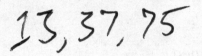

13, 37, 75

A Collective Tales Publishing Anthology

Darkness 101:
Lessons Were Learned

Cover design © 2023 by Collective Tales Publishing
Cover designed by Collective Tales Publishing
Edited by Elizabeth Suggs and Jonathan Reddoch

Contents

Introduction

Salutations, students,

Class is in session. We hope your mind is open. We present 101 unique horrifying lessons. Each trimmed down to exactly 101 unnerving words for your eerie edification.

Depicting a wide range of subjects, we visit the classics, such as vampires, mummies, and werewolves, but we also venture into the unknown and newly horrific. Like an absurd Aesop's Fable, you'll experience the faults of pupils who learn the hard way. You'll see bullies get their comeuppance. You'll witness twists and turns on a roller-coaster of misdeeds.

One thing is for certain, lessons will be learned.

Insincerely,

Your terrifying tutors

A Dark and Splintered Hole

Addison Smith

"Don't look inside."

He spread a new coat thick until it bulged from the wall. Every day the plaster chipped and every day Walter added new layers. The hole was only three inches wide, but he heeded the warning of the previous tenants to repair it.

It's just a hole in the drywall filled with dust and darkness, nothing more.

He pressed the edge of his spreader to the cracked center and frowned.

It's nonsense. What could possibly be inside?

He cut the plaster away and peered within.

It's difficult to fit a man through a three-inch hole.

The creature managed.

Relationship Resurrection

Elizabeth Suggs

Tony had promised Harriett they would be together forever. He even bought her that princess-cut ring. However, when she found him in bed with Clara, Harriett had almost called it off.

But then she solved their relationship problem by hiring a specialist.

They get along so much better now. Tony doesn't even mention Clara's name, though he doesn't say much of anything anymore. In a way, Harriett prefers his silences. She has more time to marvel at his eyes—how he looks at her like he used to with that little sparkle.

She really did hire the best taxidermist in town.

Whisked Away

Jonathan Reddoch

Joyce attended her cousin Fran's wedding sans plus one. She guzzled cheap champagne while watching giddy couples embarrass themselves on the dance floor.

Then she saw him across the ballroom. They locked eyes. They gravitated toward each other. Their hands met in perfect sync.

It was something out of a dream or an 80s music video. As the world faded away, they moved in tandem as if two halves separated by eternity.

"Want to escape this world?" his eyes whispered.

"A thousand times yes," her heartbeat answered.

He whisked her away.

That was the last time witnesses saw Joyce Crothers alive.

Just Another Flick

Chris Jorgensen

I always saw the cliché in movies and laughed. How could these teens be so stupid? How about not running into the woods screaming? It makes you a beacon in the dark!

Or perhaps don't fuck that shirtless guy in a filthy basement of an abandoned mansion? Sure, it's kinda hot to make out somewhere forbidden, but it never works out in the movies.

Maybe they should just square off with the killer by wielding a bigger weapon—how hard is that?

It doesn't work like that in the movies. The kids tied up in my basement haven't learned that lesson.

The Forest Calls

Austin Slade Perry

The village had one rule about the forest: Take what you need, but never leave your name for fear of the Fae.

I never believed in any of that. That was before the orphan Ulrick carved his name on a pine tree. The elders were disappointed but did not punish him. Perhaps they already knew his fate.

"I hear her," Ulrick whispered.

"Who?" I asked.

"Mother, she is calling me."

I couldn't stop him from running into the forest. We searched but found nothing until morning. All that was left was his iron ring and the finger he wore it on.

Timber

Alex Child

He's... real, Joe thought, back against the sawmill wall.

"I'm Barkskin, and I avenge the trees. I'll chop off your legs, and I'll never say please."

The creature's coarse bark, marred by axe scarring and droplets of sap, creaked as he approached one-handed with a rusty chainsaw.

Joe apologized, but Barkskin wasn't listening. With one passing swipe, bits of bone and shredded visceral sprayed across the stained wood walls.

"Timber!" cried Barkskin, as Joe collapsed, screaming. Barkskin picked Joe up, laying him in front of a table saw.

"Your legs will support my coffee table. And your spine, my coat rack."

The Drifter

K. R. Patterson

I sigh, receiving yet another patient's report at Sanctuary Psychiatric Hospital. The new nurse drones on about a delusional patient. She's overly concerned.

"He says he's possessed, Dr. Stevens."

"And?"

"There's darkness in him," she whispers, eyes wide. "A demon, commanding him to kill people."

I read the report. Part of my job, after all. It's nothing I haven't seen before. The gentleman is homeless.

Faker.

Interviewing the drifter, I perceive nothing unusual and discharge him. But as he approaches the exit, his demeanor morphs into a new man. A piercing laugh escapes him as he disappears into the flickering shadows.

She's My Heroin

Natalya Monyok

Muscle pulls from bone. The taste of meat, dripping with
grease. The salt on my tongue is an aphrodisiac.

When I'm done, I suck the bone marrow like a lollipop.
That spongy texture is rich with the aftertaste of death.
The adrenaline is invigorating.

I keep the bodies like souvenirs. This one I will savor
for a long time. My hardest kill yet; the result of years of
preparation, months of stalking, then, last night, an arrow
straight through the heart.

I wish I knew she had been on heroin. I have inherited this
cursed addiction, and I must hunt again.

A Father's Pride

Conor Bennett

It's not every day your son earns his mushroom identification merit badge. To give him an opportunity to demonstrate his new skill, I took him to the Wasatch Forest.

My son found a wrinkly rusted-orange mushroom.

"That's a morel!" he said.

It looked peculiar, but what kind of father would I be if I doubted him? It tasted bitter, but he insisted it was safe and healthy. As my stomach pain worsened, green bile foamed from my lips.

My son whimpered, "I'm sorry, dad, but I bought the mycology merit badge online. I just wanted you to be proud of me."

Offer

Ashley Huyge

"So, where's this party?" Candace asked, brushing a bleached curl over her shoulder. She'd never hung out with Ellie. Ellie was a shy freak, but the promise of booze and boys made their excursion into the abandoned high school buzz with possibilities.

"Just around the corner," Ellie said, her voice a nervous croak.

A low, snarling shuddered behind them.

"What was that?" Candace whimpered.

Ellie shoved Candance into a locker, trapping her inside.

"Let me out!" she cried. "Is this because I don't want to be your friend?"

"I don't need friends," Ellie backed away into the darkness. "I need sacrifices."

Reading Lessons

Brianna Malotke

The teacher said the lesson was simple: don't read ahead.
But Oliver didn't care, he wanted to read to his heart's
content. And so, after midnight, when he was supposed to
be fast asleep, he got his trusty flashlight and read under
his dinosaur covers.

He got so caught up in the material he whispered the
words out loud, reading quietly but out loud nonetheless.
His heart raced as he read, not noticing the floorboards
creaking as the demonic creature came to slurp him up. If
Oliver had waited until tomorrow, he would have learned:
never read the book out loud.

Befriending a Murder of Crows

Megan Kiekel Anderson

You scatter a handful of peanuts—an offering.

It takes time, building trust. You choose a quiet, open space. Add a bath. Establish a routine. Test treats—your new friends can be discerning. Admire them from afar; keep them wild.

They leave gifts in return. A bit of wire. A shiny new coin. A lock of hair. They grow protective, swooping down, a cacophony of calls, unable to distinguish guest from intruder. You withhold cat food—their favorite—when they scare off your lover. They learn your movements. They learn the faces of your enemies.

They leave their entrails—an offering.

Hammerschlagen

Peter L. Harmon

Last Oktoberfest you embarrassed me during the game of Hammerschlagen—that game where hammered people hammer the nail into the stump.

I wasn't very good at hammering nails. I'm more of a poet, you know, not so much one for manual labor. I missed the nail, and you laughed—chortled even. I hit the nail, and it bent. I was humiliated.

I spent the next year practicing in my garage. Nail after nail until I filled many stumps. And your Oktoberfest party is this weekend. I can't wait to bury the hammer in the middle of your forehead. That'll teach you.

Due Friday

Kelly Mintzer

Emily never did homework on Thursdays. Thursday was practically Friday and no kid should have to do homework over the weekend.

Last Thursday, Ms. O'Donnell tapped the assignment on Emily's desk. "Make sure you do your homework this time. It teaches a valuable life lesson." But Emily stuck to her principles.

Immediately after the class passed their assignments forward on Friday morning, Ms. O'Donnell turned out the lights and locked the windows.

Principal Finnegan spoke over the loudspeaker: "Children, the harvest begins now. Your homework taught you everything that you need to know to survive. Your ten-minute head start begins... now."

The Sea's Temptress

Teasha Lynn

Floating, bobbing in frosty seas, a ship's wrecked voyage,
I do see. Ten men still cling to fragments of a broken ship.
What's this? A maiden in the distance? Probably a delirious
distraction of the mind.

Closer she draws to our luckless men. Is this some sign?
Some merciful salvation?

Closer still, she moves; her beauty is beyond compare. She
slinks up to the strongest man and sweetly whispers promis-
es of bliss.

Such tempting words he could not resist, so he takes her
hand. A foolish slip and fatal lesson for the rest. For, desper-
ate men are a mermaid's favorite meal.

Anything for Tenure

Nicholas Yanes

Wilkes desired tenure more than anything. She had sacrificed relationships and other career opportunities. Though she had wanted a family, all she had was a wilting Ficus. But after all her recent articles were rejected from top-tier journals, tenure seemed increasingly out of reach.

Derivative. Unoriginal. Rehashed. These words kept reappearing in her letters.

The editor of *Medieval Lore*, sensing her desperation, offered access to a book with pages cut from human flesh, words inked in crimson.

She ignored the warnings, spilled her blood, and summoned dark knowledge.

Though tenured, she remained forever trapped in a body puppeteered by a demon.

My Lips Are Sealed

AudraKate Gonzalez

"Don't touch me!" Tanya yelled. She didn't understand why Brett couldn't get it through his big head. She was not interested.

"Come on, sweetheart. Just one date." Brett reached out, grabbing her arm.

"I said don't touch me. And I am not your sweetheart," Tanya seethed through her teeth. The audacity of this entitled douchebag!

"I know how I can make you say yes." Brett grabbed her by the waist and leaned in for a kiss.

With a flick of her wrist, Tanya sealed Brett's mouth closed for good. Brett screamed, pulling at his lips.

"I'm sorry! I can't hear you."

Sacrifices
Were Made

Kristy Lytle

Bridgette nervously peeks over the cliffside where waves violently crash against the jagged rocks below. Her long blonde hair dances wildly around her face with each gust of wind.

"I'm really scared," she says to her new friend, Sylvia.

"You must remind yourself this is necessary for freedom," Sylvia replies.

Bridgette sighs and looks into Sylvia's dark eyes. She gives a short, determined nod then leaps from the cliff.

"Hail Satan!" she screams as she plummets to her watery grave.

Sylvia peers over the cliff and cackles as she watches Bridgette slam into the cold, rocky sea below.

"Idiot," Sylvia mutters.

Banquet

Robin Knabel

The tour guide warned me, but I didn't believe in folklore.

Dense forest consumed me. I thought I'd been bitten by
an insect when the first dart hit my arm. The second struck
my neck, the feathered barb dangling.

Trees blurred as bodies that were painted like skeletons
danced around me.

The first slice felt like a deep scratch. More followed, and
a frenzy erupted as pronged forks dug into me, twisting
and gouging my muscles.

Strips of raw flesh hung from my limbs like fringe; my
skin burning like fire.

Hoarse, I surrendered.

Darkness fell, and I was no more.

Locked From the Outside

Taylor Crook

The shadow, Sam's nightly visitor, coalesces in the corner of the ceiling.

It's nothing at first, a trick of the eye.

Slowly, mist becomes muscle, slinking across the ceiling.

Soon, it will be directly above Sam. It's hungry.

Sam isn't sure what happens then. He's never let it get that far. He always runs to his parents' room and climbs in their bed, his gentle sobs fading until sleep takes him.

But not tonight. Tonight, he can't leave. Father told him to be brave. To face his fears.

His parents don't believe him. Neither does the doctor. Come morning, they will.

Sexual Harassment

Jo Birdwell

He squeezed her ass a few times, would stare down her shirt, and said things like "nice tits." Nurse Nancy kept telling him to stop.

He'd been in the hospital for days. He was bored. She was hot. He grabbed her chest as she leaned over him. She stormed off, returning a minute later with a large needle.

She approached his bedside, smiling.

To Scott's horror, she injected a thick clear substance into his vein. His muscles tensed and his eyes bulged as he screamed. Staring down at him, still smiling, she watched as Scott's eyes closed and his breathing slowed.

Library Meet Cute

Jonathan Reddoch

Richard, a doctoral candidate in ancient cultic symbology, reached up for the sole intact first edition of *Armand's Encyclopedia of Death Runes*.

As he did so, the tattooed green fingers of Marija, president of the Alpha Centauri Telesticial Society, grasped the dusty tome.

"Excuse me!" Richard said, "I need this for my research!"

"Pardon me, it's for ACTS initiation. Club rush this weekend; we need new blood."

"But…"

"Yes?" she smiled crossly.

"Get a room you two," interjected the MU librarian. They blushed. She amended, "A *study* room to share the book."

The scholars sniggered. The librarian guffawed. The encyclopedia cackled.

Blemish

Alex Child

The body-length antique mirror highlighted a blemish he had never seen before. Just to the right of his nose was a bulbous, crimson abomination jutting from his face like an overgrown barnacle.

He squeezed it between his fingers, stinging his cheeks, but it remained utterly unaffected no matter how hard he pressed.

He needed it gone. He just did.

Every failed attempt raised his agony, until eventually, he stood in front of his haggard reflection with a knife, cutting away at his own skin.

But the mirror didn't show the blood dripping from his chiseled face. It only showed the blemish.

Mom's Always Right

H. V. Patterson

The abandoned lot was full of old junk, broken appliances, and even a few rusting cars. Billy wasn't supposed to play there, especially alone. But his friends were at camp, and he couldn't spend another minute inside with his screaming, teething little brother.

Billy climbed into a grimy refrigerator and closed the door. He pretended he was a space explorer in hibernation, waiting to discover strange new worlds.

It got hard to breathe. Billy pushed, but he couldn't force the fridge door back open.

I should've listened to Mom, he thought as stars danced across his vision, and he lost consciousness.

A Lover's Truth

Austin Slade Perry

His touch, which had once soothed me, now felt like frost wrapping over my skin. His once low voice now echoed with a deep hungry growl. But what truly scared me was that his bright blue eyes were now a dark pit, pulling me in.

Why have I never seen it before? Had my desire blinded me from the truth of his own dark desires? From his true nature?

If I had seen it, would it have made a difference? Would I've been able to escape him? Never having to feel the bittersweet sensation of his teeth plunging into my neck?

Thank the Lord!

Elizabeth Suggs

Sister Marland had the wire hanger out again. Another child was saved.

The sister spotted me and tightened her grip along the rusty bent metal. It was said girls get infected with sin if she stared long enough, but I didn't care because I was already corrupted. I liked watching her wrinkled skin tighten and twist. Her frown deepened and no sooner had I stepped up to her had she grabbed my shoulder and thrust me into a room rank with blood.

"Evil infects you." She shoved me on a stained mattress and lifted the hanger. "It must be purged. Hallelujah!"

Home Invasion

Ethan Reisler

A delinquent squeezed through boarded windows, entering my home with spray paint in hand and vandalism in mind. Stories of a spirit roaming my halls brought him here, like many before, and will bring others long after him. They bring apathy and leave their hate, destroying anything they want. They've already burned my west wing to ash.

This insolent child was no different, intruding without a second thought—he needed to be made an example of. I ground his eyes to jelly and salted his muscles like pork, using his blood to paint the newest warning in the entryway: "NO TRESPASSING."

There's Nothing Under the Bed

Nina Tolstoy

My head on the pillow, sheets up to my chin—*there's nothing under the bed.*

But what's that sound?

Sounds of scratching and gnawing, like a monster or something undead. Faint at first, then louder and louder, scraping claws and gnashing teeth. A whisper calls, "come to me, child." The voice pierces the blanket I hide underneath.

My scream stops in my throat, but I manage to yell, "There's no monsters under my bed!" The laughter comes next, that familiar laughter, and a cold, creeping hiss that says, "But, child, I'm from the closet. Of course, there's nothing under your bed."

Package

Joshua G. J. Insole

I'll make them pay, Cassian thought.

They all laughed at him and called his ideology *backward* and his logic *flawed*. They'd suggested he was a few pieces short of a jigsaw—they'd humiliated him. But now, they would regret calling him *stupid*.

His letterbox rattled with the mail. Junk mail and circulars, along with several small brown boxes. Had he seen something this size and shape before? Even the handwriting rang a distant bell in the back of his mind.

One final thought sliced through his brain before the darkness: *Why did I put a return address on the letter bombs?*

Glass Half Empty

Chris Jorgensen

My friends warned me it was a cult. I should have believed them. The midnight ceremony that took place
really started to emphasize that. In some fairness, I had
no idea that it was going to turn out this way, but when
they brought out a woman stripped naked and placed on a
stone table, eyes open, unable to move, barely breathing
as it was, all the pieces sort of clicked together. When they
drained her blood and passed the golden goblet around for
everyone, it became obvious that I had joined a cult.

When you are this deep, you drink.

Radio Silence

P. S. Tom

Derrick takes a sip of coffee. He starts the car, and the headlights switch on.

"Missing girl discovered by her dog after months of being locked in her neighbor's home. The perpetrator is still at large."

Click.

He shuts the radio off.

"Wow!" he says as he pulls away. "If she was next door for months and no one knew, how many people are tied up in basements now? How many are never found?" Gazing out the window his mind wanders.

After a few hours, he pulls into a driveway. "Fucking dog! Won't make that mistake again." He pops the trunk.

Just One Spoonful More

Brianna Malotke

She woke up with a natural smile. At last, she felt at peace. No loud yelling, no lingering muscle aches. The sun seemed brighter, eclipsing all of the darkness that had once inhabited her home. She moved through the old Victorian manor with a spring in her step.

The silence blanketing the residence was so unusual, but welcomed. She loved every minute of this new solitude, dancing around, doing whatever she pleased. It had taken a few tries, but she had finally figured out the way to be free from him.

Finally tasting freedom, her secret: arsenic in their sugar jar.

Make a Wish

McKenzie Richardson

No coins, read the sign at the edge of the pond.

But everyone knows such places hold magic! There are wishes to be granted, dreams to make true.

Sam put her back to the pool, squeezed the penny as she made her wish, then flipped it over her shoulder. It landed with a splendid *plop*.

Drip, drop.

Sam spun at the unexpected noise. A woman stood in the pond, scraggly hair dripping.

From between her jagged, yellow teeth, a penny tumbled, landing at Sam's feet.

"A rule breaker," the woman growled. "It seems my wish came true. I was getting hungry."

Tome of Reflection

Katie Collupy

The dusty tome sat before the librarian.

Her hand hovered over the weathered cover, ready to flip to the first page. An ominous feeling crept over her. The book had been locked away behind glass for eons, but her urge to learn the ancient ways was too strong.

A scream pierced the air as she opened it. It was not until her eyes landed on the horrifying reflection within the pages that she realized she was the one screaming.

She tried to snap the book shut, but it resisted. A decomposing hand grabbed her by the wrist and dragged her inside.

Spider Queen

Ashley Huyge

I believe in spirit guides. Mine is the spider. Spiders are everywhere, following me, protecting me, serving me. Today, they reveal who stole my sister's bike.

I watch them clustering above Leslie during a life cycle documentary in biology class. In the darkness, all eyes are on the screen while a constellation of spiders grows above us.

I could tap on her shoulder and point up. But I decide not to warn her.

They sprinkle down, like motes of dust, but she doesn't scream—not until the big ones fall in her hair and start biting.

Revenge is better than justice.

In the Sand

Austin Slade Perry

In the sand, we found his tomb. And our fortune. The locals warned us of the ancient curse. We took it as a foolish superstition, but soon, we learned *we* were the fools.

Within the following months, I watched as my team succumbed to his spell. They dropped like flies, infected with a plague believed to be long dormant.

Now I'm all that's left.

I can't sleep. I know he's coming. His eyeless sockets haunt my every thought. I feel his dry breath down my neck. He's toying with my suffering.

In the sand, I found his tomb. And my doom.

Dr. Frankenstein's Monster's Monster

Peter L. Harmon

Look.

We know that the big fella with rotting greenish skin, black hair, and bolts in his neck, with the shabby clothing and the strange gait. Big shoes, clunky boots with a bit of a heel. We know that his name is NOT Frankenstein. Frankenstein is the doctor, and the aforementioned lumbering giant stitched together from a collage of corpses is Dr. Frankenstein's monster.

We've been reminded of this fact many times. We get it.

HOWEVER!

What happens when that monster creates his own abomination to mankind and sets it loose in the castle with the intent of destroying Dr. Frankenstein?

DIY Shampoo

Elizabeth Suggs

"You threw away my homemade shampoo?" Katie yelled at Clare. "I need it for my skin condition!"

"Condition-smitchen! It stunk up the bathroom with pickles and farts! No wonder no guy will come within ten yards of you." Clare handed Katie a new plastic bottle of Pantomime Pro-bee shampoo. "You can borrow mine until you buy something that doesn't smell like shit."

Their argument was interrupted by a howl in the distance.

It was too late.

Without her special shampoo to conceal her tempting scent, her lupine lovers would track her down.

That's what she gets for accepting a new roommate.

A Visit from the Elders

Jonathan Reddoch

Two pale figures in dark suits knocked at the door.

An old man in a robe answered, "It's dinner time; what do you want?"

"Ve vant to introduce ourselves. Ve're representatives of our lord and master, who suffered and died for the sins of his followers. Ve're sharing a message about his death and resurrection dis evening. He offers us his divine gift of immortality and eternal life. May ve come in?"

"We're atheists."

His wife chimed in from the living room, "But we could use a good laugh…"

"Are you inviting us in?"

"Sure, come in. Let's hear your spiel."

Awakening

K. R. Patterson

I wake in darkness. Cushioned. Confined. Claustrophobic. Perhaps it's my breath coming back to meet me.

As I finger the too-close walls, I know where I am.

My last known memory was crossing a street. White lines. Red numbers counting down. That's it.

I panic. *I've been buried alive!*

But then… peace. A distant recollection. A printed slip from a fortune-telling machine promised, "You will live forever."

My thoughts are numb, focused only on one thing: my hunger.

I break through the coffin and climb through the dirt with ease, as if swimming.

There's only one thought on my mind: *Brains*.

Terms of Service

Conor Bennett

Making deals for souls used to be so much fun. Meeting face-to-face at crossroads, deals struck in moonlight. Even the occasional fiddle duel here and there. Now it's all so corporate; everything is done behind a computer screen.

At least the best part hasn't changed. That part will never change. Flaying the skin of damned souls, grinding their teeth, witnessing their despair. But even I'll admit that we have never seen this number of souls before. I just miss the art of it. Nowadays, it's as simple as creating an app.

When will people learn to read the terms of service?

Solve for X

Thomas S. Salem

Senior Chester Brigham held freshman Ronnie Clarke by the neck of his shirt. Both were surrounded by students from the high school.

"Ready for your after-school beatdown?" Brigham growled.

The crowd laughed.

"Ready for your after-school lesson?"

The crowd gasped. This was the first time the math nerd talked back to the bully.

"What?"

Ronnie then pulled out a pair of scissors and opened the blades in an X. "How do you solve for X?"

"I hate algebra!"

Ronnie thrust the scissors forward into his skull. "With your brain!" He laughed.

Everybody left that afternoon understanding how to solve for *X*.

Night Crawling

Peter Hayward-Bailey

Minerva woke to something tickling her arm. A big prickly spider scurried up her bicep, toward her neck.

She swiped at it, knocking it to the floor. Minerva grabbed a book from her bedside table and crushed it with a satisfying crunch as it tried to make an escape.

She drew in a sharp breath as something stroked her feet. She pulled back the covers and hundreds of the thin-limbed spiders were crawling out from under the bed. Before she could move, they were all over her, covering every inch of her skin. She screamed, and they swarmed her every crevice.

School Doesn't Stop

AudraKate Gonzalez

"You've got to be kidding me!" I gripped the seat in front of me tighter as the bus shifted back and forth. I could not believe my parents signed the permission slip.

"Life still has to go on," Bonnie said as a loud explosion shook the bus.

"Hang on, everybody! The tremors will hit," the bus driver announced. Outside the window, a building collapsed. Thankfully, it was in the quarantine section, so nobody was inside.

"I understand that life has to go on, but a field trip? Really?" I wished we could stay home. Permanently.

"School doesn't stop for alien invasions."

Urban Legend

Gully Novaro

Mrs. Darcy, the lady who lives down the street, has a secret.

She is cooking right now, she knows this toffee recipe that is to die for. But that's not it.

She cuts twelve golden pieces, and wraps them in colored wax paper. So pretty they can kill. But that's not it.

Tonight, she will be out, walking with the trick or treaters. She has tricks to play tonight, to those who break the rules, and with the skill of an assassin, she'll sneak them a treat.

That's her secret.

The candy they warn you about, with the hidden razor blades.

The New Boy

Paul Lonardo

Walking through the woods, a brother and sister encountered a strange boy sitting on a rock wall. They had never seen his dark freckled face before.

"Hell's just on the other side," the boy said with a wily grin.

"Liar," Aaron told him. "There's no such thing as Hell."

"Hell's a make-believe place invented to scare people," Emily added.

"Why don't you look for yourself," the boy said.

"I will," Aaron said.

"Be careful," Emily cautioned.

Aaron ascended the wall with ease. Waving, he disappeared over the edge. After the screaming stopped, Emily never heard from Aaron or the boy again.

Fresh Apricots

Alex Child

Darla pulled over to the fruit stand. Apricots were in season, and though he was eccentric, the salesman assured her that these were the freshest apricots she would ever eat.

She took a bite as she drove away.

The nectar swarmed her taste buds in euphoria. She opened her mouth for another bite as one of her front teeth clattered to the car floor.

But... it didn't hurt.

And even if it did, she would have continued.

Darla kept eating, teeth littering the floor of her car. When the last fell, she only regretted that she couldn't finish the remaining apricots.

Too Late

Robin Knabel

Joe told me not to go, that it was a prank.

My head swims with libations and flirtations. Dainty fingers push pills between my slack lips before kissing them shut.

Music pounds; I drift away. A cradle of hands is beneath me, guiding me. Whispers carry on the breeze, my name intertwined with laughter, shushing. Cold soil embraces me with its crumbling walls of dirt and moss.

I gasp, thick earth filling my mouth. I cannot scream. Eyes open wide, heavy ground pressing against me. I think of Joe as I surrender to the darkness.

I should have listened to him.

No Trespassing

Nina Tolstoy

Her previous creations watched nonchalantly, glass marbles staring as she prepared her latest work of art. This one a fox that had dared enter her territory, threatening her birds.

"That'll learn you." She chuckled, stripping the fur of its flesh, stuffing the empty sack of skin, giving him form. She hadn't done this in years. Arthritic fingers, weak sight, but she hadn't lost her touch.

She searched her drawers for suitable eyes, finding only brown.

"Green would be better!" She discarded the eyes.

The doorbell rang. She answered it, annoyed. A salesman, with shocking green eyes.

"Come in." She smiled greedily.

Psych 101

Jo Birdwell

Cody's lawyer got him off easy with an insanity plea for the Hawthorne County Murders.

He loathed the psych ward! But a short stint here, faking the "crazies," trumped life behind bars.

Nurse Val glowered when he walked in.

She led him back to a patient room. As the door closed, he felt a sharp jab in his neck. He sank to the floor.

Cody awoke, restrained, something cold and metallic on his head; Nurse Val stood over him.

"Now you'll really be crazy!" she cackled.

He shook violently as electricity pulsed throughout his brain, strong enough to drive anyone mad.

Champain Room

Taylor Crook

Jade straddled his lap as eighties glam rock pulsed around him. She smiled at Tony, but he didn't remember how he got there... *I don't frequent strip clubs.*

Well, just that once...

"I don't..." Tony began and tried to get up.

"*Shhh.*"

"My wife..."

Jade smiled too widely. Needle-sharp teeth tore into flesh. Then, there was pain.

Not the pain of rending flesh, but a deeper pain. A pain borne of sorrow and shame that flowed out of Tony. Even as he remembered, he knew he would forget.

It was just one mistake. *Right?*

"See you soon."

He knew she would.

Tell, Don't Show

Jenifer Schwendiman

He wrinkled his nose at the mildew in the refrigerator. It was over a month since it was cleaned. Just like his laundry stinking up his room.

He opened his diary and flipped through the pages that documented the ups and downs of his first relationship. His parents didn't understand how much it hurt to be betrayed by true love. He had tried to show them his exact feelings, but now they didn't even buy food or wash his clothes. He reflected that perhaps some things, like the overwhelming feeling of being stabbed in the heart, are best told, not shown.

No Fishing

Kristy Lytle

Murky water laps up the side of the dinghy. Meera leans over and eyes the water suspiciously. "Are you sure it's safe? That sign back there said *no fishing in the lake…*"

Brent scoffs, "Babe, it's fine. Just settle down."

Meera rolls her eyes as she casts her first line. Almost immediately, there's a tug.

"I've got something big!"

The rod violently rips from her hands, disappearing under water.

They peer over the boat's ledge to see an enormous shadow moving rapidly upwards. Screams are cut short as leviathan jaws burst out of the water, swallowing the boat and couple whole.

Deification of a Mad God

H. V. Patterson

"At last!" cackled Dr. Robertson. "I have it! Immortality and godhood in my hands!"

He opened the forbidden book made of human skin. As he chanted the arcane words, he transformed. His skin bubbled and boiled away, and his bones crumbled to dust inside him. He chanted, even as his lips melted, his skull imploded, and his tongue flopped to the ground.

When the chant ended, all that remained of Dr. Robertson was a pile of pulsating muscle and fat, topped with oozing brains.

But Dr. Robertson was still aware. Immortal, all-knowing, and condemned to eternal agony, he soon went mad.

Too Late to Leave Narrabri

Peter V. Hilton

Tuesday's issue of *The Courier* landed on the veranda, reduced to *The Cour*— by the unseen rodents before I even woke. Those hundred bite marks ended my limbo.

The nesting has come to Narrabri, I reckoned. Paper in hand, I settled down to wait.

Three nights come and gone, and the house fares no better than the paper. In tonight's skittering darkness, the floors are an undulating mass of mangy fur and tiny, tiny teeth.

Before bed, I rang cousin Jermaine to say goodbye, but the line died, severed by the all-consuming nest. Any second now, any second, and I'll be—

More than Halfway to Madness

Aiden E. Messer

Hello, dear reader,

You probably think that what you are reading is just a book. That's your first mistake. Can you feel it already? The echo of a headache, tiredness, and the urge to yawn? You might believe that it's nothing, a simple coincidence. This is your second mistake. What you are feeling right now, dear reader, are the early signs of your mind tearing itself into 101 pieces, ready to scatter beyond the limits of reality. You've just read many stories about harsh consequences. You are now living your own.

Words are powerful, and you shouldn't trust books so easily.

Follow the Rules

Morgana Price

1. Stay behind the counter.

2. Never answer the phone.

3. Always say, "Thank you for coming in!" after finishing a transaction.

4. When the lights go out, please recite, "Mary had a Little Lamb."

    a. Clapping means you are safe.

    b. No clapping? Leave the gas station immediately!

I scoff at the rules. Graveyard shifts equal easy money. A guy walks in and buys a soda.

"You didn't thank me," he says.

He grabs my throat. He has no face. I squeak out an apology. He releases me and slowly leaves.

The lights turn out, but I've lost my voice.

I don't hear clapping.

Shallow

Chris Jorgensen

Halloween was supposed to be a time for fun and festivities. But when the call goes out in our small woodland community that someone's gone missing you join the search party. What kind of monster wouldn't help?

We called through the woods on the outskirts of town, looking for any sign of the missing girl. People combed through the foliage with a one-hundred-foot stretch between them, all in the dire hope of finding her.

So many people in this patch of woods, someone has to discover her.

Luckily, I made sure I was the one to pass over her shallow grave.

Green Eyes

Natalya Monyok

Glowing green eyes skittered in the darkness ahead. But the monsters were blind, so I was safe if I stayed silent. I trekked onwards carefully.

But the soldiers closed in behind me, forcing me to venture deeper into the ominous forest. They barked orders that I was to be killed on sight.

As the soldiers grew closer, so too did the monsters' growls. I quickly scaled a tree, but a soldier heard me, raised his weapon, and ordered me to halt. But it was too late for him and his noisy compatriots. The green eyes descended, the monsters devouring them whole.

An Overwhelming Surprise

Elizabeth Suggs

"Thanks for calling. I know you're busy," Davis said. The old man was elated to hear from his estranged son.

"Actually, I called about a letter Stephanie mailed. Did you read it?" Scott said.

"Steph's forgiven me?"

After decades of neglect, Davis' children had lost contact. A letter from his beloved daughter Stephanie was an overwhelming surprise.

He clutched his chest.

"It's a brochure for a retirement home. Stephanie thinks you'd do better there, and I agree. Dad?" Scott said, but his words had fallen on deaf ears. Davis had fallen on the ground. The heart attack had proved instantly fatal.

Love Spell

AudraKate Gonzalez

"It was a harmless love spell. I picked it up from that herbal shop on Main. I doubt it works anyway." I rolled my eyes at Stephanie.

"You don't think it'll work on Mack?"

I shrugged my shoulders. "I put it in his hydro flask."

Just then, Mack rounded the corner. He barely noticed me.

"Hey, Mack." I batted my eyelashes at him. "Did you stay hydrated today?"

"Actually, I didn't go to practice, so I gave my Gatorade to the other guys. They really loved it!"

"What?!" I screamed.

Then the entire football team came chasing me down the hall.

Cutting Edge Weight Loss

Conor Bennett

Always leave your fingers for last. How else could you handle the knife to slice the tender bits of meat, strip the bone? My calf was tougher than my thigh, but the meat scraped off the bone easier. I've been bedridden due to my extreme weight for years. I had relied on the kindness of others to live but haven't been visited for weeks.

"You gotta work your way up from the bottom," Dad always taught. If only he could see me now. Left to rot. Forgotten. I've always wanted to be skin and bones. I'll settle for just the bones.

My Father's Lesson

Austin Slade Perry

Father taught me everything I know. He was a great hunter after all. He showed me how to track, how to trap, and most importantly, how to kill. He taught me how to skin my prey, gut it, cook it, and eat it.

As I grew older, my taste for the sport became more refined. I needed something more appealing, challenging, and appetizing.

Then I saw you. The perfect prey.

Oh, I knew it would be a challenge, but that's what excited me.

Shhh, don't cry. My father taught me well; you will be the finest meal that I've ever devoured.

The Dip

D. J. James

The bully brought the geek into the bathroom stall, one covered in filth and graffiti. In fanatical rage, the bully planned on shoving the geek's head deep into the toilet.

"Ready for a dip, pussy?" he asked, sneering.

The geek struggled against the bully's tight grip as they edged closer to the bowl. The bully shoved the geek to his knees, and the geek begged him to stop.

Once he put the geek's head into the water, squid-like tentacles came out, grabbed the bully, and pulled him in, the bully vanished almost instantly.

The geek, surprised, got up and ran away.

The Elf

Paul Lonardo

The first time James forgot to move Slide, the Christmas elf, James had fallen asleep on the couch, martini in hand. Yet Slide had found its way from the floor lamp to the television stand. His wife denied responsibility, and his daughter Vicky was too small to reach it.

On Christmas Eve, James passed out in a drunken stupor again. The next morning, there was no sign of Slide.

A pitter-pattering of tiny feet drew James into the kitchen, where Slide jumped down onto his shoulders and skewered his eyeballs with plastic cocktail swords and plopped them into James' martini glass.

Last Dance

Ashley Huyge

Andrea stumbled into the silver dappled gym, her head throbbing. She remembered begging her date not to drink in the car, the screech of tires, but not arriving at the school.

She drifted across the pulsing dance floor, calling to her friends. Why were they ignoring her? Screaming their names had no effect. Then she caught her reflection in the window.

The skin of her forehead tore away from her scalp, blood soaking her pink gown.

Her date appeared beside her like a mist in the darkness.

"Why didn't we cross over?" she asked.

"I didn't want you to miss Prom."

One Final Scare

F. Malanoche

Heidi's penchant for playing hide-and-seek with her teacher was unrivaled. She would sit in the darkest spot she could find until Mrs. Bellwether grew sick with worry. Only when the old lady's voice would quiver with fear would the young girl spring forth.

Heidi found a pitch-black crevice to hide in. Though the heat grew with each passing minute, she stayed still. She loved to frighten that horrible old bat. Today would prove to be her last chance to play.

She would learn her lesson too late: some games are not meant on a field trip, especially one to the crematorium.

Stockholm

K. R. Patterson

"I'm here to give you a gift," said the bespectacled man who kidnapped me. He violated my body until I eventually gave in. He grew nicer over time, but still, the word "gift" chilled me. Until he began to release not one, but all of my shackles.

He even said I could leave. But if I did, he'd kill himself before the authorities arrived.

No. I couldn't let that happen.

The stories he told me. His life. Some just to entertain, others helped me understand his pain. Time passed until it finally struck me. I cared for him.

My only friend.

Galatea's Bird Cage

Anne Gregg

Galatea was enchanting to watch. She kept calm under the harsh yellow light of her cage. Her fingers tapped the one-way glass, testing it. When the experiments began, she remained curious. Her hands traced my window to her.

"Soon," I whispered, "soon."

Even as the trials fatigued her, she endured for me, my sculpted angel.

On her final day, her strength returned. I was ecstatic as she leaned into me, into the glass.

Then her fist shattered it. Her hand punctured my chest and pulled out my beating heart. She bit into it as I hit the floor, stealing my love.

Left Unsaid

Gully Novaro

I talk about dreams, yours, mine, and ours. About the paths we want to take and how we would end up drifting apart. Different goals.

A tear falls from your eye, I use my thumb to wipe it out. I tell you not to cry, this isn't a goodbye. Maybe that's how it sounds, but I want us to be together for the rest of our lives. I hold your hand and you hold mine; we look into each other's eyes.

"Til the end," I say, as I raise my glass.

I never tell you about the poison in the wine.

Freshmeat Prank

Jonathan Reddoch

Bridger snuck out behind the cafeteria for a smoke. The teachers were too busy on their coffee break to notice.

"Help," whispered a small voice from inside the dumpster.

Bridger stuck his nose in, got a big whiff, but couldn't see anyone.

"Freshmeat prank?" Bridger laughed, fondly recalling his own freshman hazing.

"Help. You. Help, in here, quickly," the still small voice urged.

Bridger laughed, knowing this rite of passage was for his own benefit. "Sorry, can't help you."

A grim voice bellowed from above, "The child wasn't seeking assistance… they were offering sanctuary."

Then the floating specter swallowed Bridger's face.

The Truth

Abby Bathurst

That day was the worst of my life.

Never had I felt so alone, isolated from the rest of the world,
especially from my loved ones, Sophie, John, and Rue.

It was poetic, really, how tragically beautiful it was.
Orange and pink hues blended with my darkened skin,
morphing into a sunset silhouette. My wrists were encir-
cled by silver bracelets, biting my flesh.

Distant shouts from loved ones echoed into my ears as
they bounced off the stone walls. Darkness encased my
body. It was then that I realized life's cruel lesson: no matter what happens, you will end up alone.

Litterbug

McKenzie Richardson

A wrapper fluttered to the ground.

"Hey!" shouted the woman on the porch. "Pick up your damn garbage. Don't leave it in my yard!"

The girl glared from beneath red sunglasses. "Bug off!" she snarled, then sauntered toward the schoolyard.

A shock of light burst from the woman's fingertip, slamming into the girl's back. Antennas sprouted from her skull, a second pair of appendages poked from her sides, and her body shrank to the size of a golf ball. The newly-formed insect scuttled through the throng of homeroom-bound children, frantically darting their crushing feet.

The woman sneered. "Nobody likes a litterbug."

Held After Class

Margaret Gaffney

Being held five minutes after class was not how George thought to begin his Friday afternoon. He glanced out the window to see the city bus pulling away. Charlie would have to find someone else to play third base. If he made it to the game, he'd have to sit with the losers in the bleachers anyway.

"Teasing others is not tolerated here." Mr. Ferguson's voice brought George's eyes back to him.

"No, sir." George frowned. He could've been a professional third baseman one day.

Mr. Ferguson sighed, extracting the meat cleaver from his top drawer. "What hand will it be?"

Crab Thief

Peter L. Harmon

Maryland crabs are expensive. I don't blame ya for not
wanting to pay for a bushel down at the shack.

It was easier to sneak out on your boat before dawn and
lift my crab pots. Even easier to get a couple friends back
to your apartment to feast. Beer cans are popping open.
Old Bay spilling onto your dirty carpet.

I can smell you steaming them now, and they smell good.

I'm under your bed waiting for your friends to leave. I'm
gonna take a crab mallet to your knees, and then use you
as bait to catch more crabs.

A Cheat Sheet to Hell

Nicholas Yanes

Desperation. Entitlement. Laziness. The three excuses for students failing to study for exams. Professor Aster should have simply flunked these students, but instead she found use for them.

After all, every soul she collected earned her another year of life.

So, she scattered cheat sheets throughout campus and on message boards. Hungry for unearned success, students ignored the fine details completely unrelated to course material.

Students assumed that the words they didn't understand were scientific terms they had never come across; they didn't realize they were reading a Faustian contract in a dead language:

Comedent animam meam.

Translation: *Eat my soul.*

Proof

Joshua G. J. Insole

Kyla put her hands on her hips and stood her ground.

Shaun blew a raspberry. "No way!"

"But it's true!"

"Liar, liar, pants on fire!"

Tears sparkled in her bright eyes. "I'm not lying!"

"Nuh-uh! Prove it!"

Kyla looked him up and down, then stuck her chin out. "Hmph. You'll be saying sorry when I prove you wrong."

Shaun rolled his eyes but followed her from his dad's apartment to the one Kyla shared with her mom on the floor above. The balcony was thirty feet high. Tiny hands gripped the railing.

Alas, her theory proved incorrect.

She could not fly.

Shoehorn

Jonathan Reddoch

A middle-aged woman returned home from the market. But the house wasn't right. The meatloaf on the table was stale. The forks were set on the left. The goblet was filled with red, not white, wine.

The rug was stained. The curtains were dark. The candles burned bright.

The faces in the portraits were foreign. The face in the mirror was false. The woman in her bed was old and miserable.

They shook each other awake. "Get out of my house!" they shouted in unison.

Throttling each other's throats one said, "One of us is—"

"Dead."

But which was which?

What to Expect

Alex Child

"It's itching, and I've been hearing things," I said.

The doctor nodded, pressing a medical instrument against my ear with an indifferent "Hmm." My ear lit with irritation, and I winced, wishing to heaven I could scratch it.

"Apologies—think I scared it."

"Scared... what?"

The doctor grinned.

"You're the perfect incubator. Consistent body temperature, young enough to hold plenty of eggs."

I bolted upright, accidentally tearing off the paper that covered the exam table. "What are you talking about?"

An insectoid limb sprouted from the side of the doctor's head and waved.

"It won't be long now," he said, smiling.

After Hours Entity

Morgana Price

My sister and I pace the halls after sundown—live bait for the entity.

"Quiet so far. Maybe it didn't hide here," I say.

No response.

Glancing over my shoulder, my blood freezes.

The entity took her body minus the eyes. Only skeletal shadows stare back at me.

I back away slowly, never averting my gaze. I grab my phone and dial the paranormal extraction team. "I see it. One casualty."

It smiles broadly with razors for teeth.

"Location?"

"Howard Elementary," I say.

It scowls.

My heart aches for my sister, but I can't look away, lest I be taken too.

For God and Country

Ashley Huyge

"If I enlist, I start after graduation?" Liam asks the army recruitment officer.

Olivia holds Liam's hand but can't stand to look at him. Grandma always said she had the gift of second sight, but why hadn't she seen he was a cheater? She wanted to break up, but grandma said wait.

"Liv? I know you have a weird sense about the future. Will I die overseas?"

Olivia closes her eyes. She sees explosions. She hears him cry, "Mommy!" She watches his red glistening intestines spill out of his body, twisting in the dirt.

"No," she smiles, "you should sign up."

Revelation

Robin Knabel

The sound is deafening as the burst of fire sears through my chest. In disbelief, I dig my finger into the warm, seeping wound.

Hands push my shoulders, and I'm falling backward, the cold water shocking me when I break the surface. Bubbles rise from my mouth as I scream into the growing darkness. I glide downward, like a leaf on the breeze falling to rot and decay.

Hair fans out around my head, and I wonder if I look beautiful. Blood red ribbons spiral upwards.

My eyes close as the gentle water rocks me to sleep.

Who will miss me?

Those Who Dig

McKenzie Richardson

The neighborhood squirrels dig up the yard, storing food for winter. They forget where over half are stored. That's how new trees grow.

I like digging too. But unlike the squirrels, I remember where everything's buried.

Theo is under the hawthorn tree. Cadence is next to the rose bushes. Bryan is beneath the porch.

When I came home from school today, I found landscapers digging in the yard. Father wants an inground pool.

I'll be adding him to the collection soon, in the hole the workers dug. Father should have known better than to rip up the yard without consulting me.

Beneath the Skin

Nina Tolstoy

"Useless witch!" She peered into the mirror scornfully at her near-perfect face.

"Beauty is beneath the skin?! I didn't want that fraudster's platitudes; I wanted results."

Just one tiny flaw, that was all.

"She knows nothing about beauty! Disgusting hag."

Her fingernails scratched at the skin. As she picked at the spot on her cheek, a small bead of blood blossomed. But a new imperfection appeared by the first. She picked it off too, compelled. It felt good to remove the offending flesh. Only a moment passed, before another two formed.

"It must be even." She bled and continued to pick.

Bully

Peter Hayward-Bailey

Tony waited for Kat after gymnastics. She was short and thin—easy prey. And if she did fight back, it usually didn't take too much roughing up for him to get what he wanted.

Kat was rushing home from school before it got dark, stopping dead when she saw him.

"I want your phone!" he spat, pushing her against the wall.

"Not today; I don't have time!" she said, pushing against his massive form.

"Hand it over!" he demanded.

Darkness fell, and Kat raised a claw that had moments ago been just a hand. Nails ripped flesh, and the bully fell.

Screaming Your Name

Elizabeth Suggs

I stare out at the haunting sea; the waves crash and churn, begging for me to step over that cliff to join you. Sometimes you whisper to me in the wind, as if I could answer, as if your death hadn't stolen my words, as if I hadn't yelled at you and made you slip over the edge. You cursed me with your last breath, and I promised I would make recompense, but until now, I've been too afraid to keep my vow.

Silenced for my sin, I'll find my voice as I plummet to your outstretched arms, screaming your name.

Supplementary

Joshua G. J. Insole

Estelle displayed the bright pink medicine bottle.

"It's an all-natural dietary supplement. I found it online! You take one, and the pounds just disappear." She tapped some pills into her palm. The other ladies *oohed* and *ahhed*. "Go ahead, try one."

Each woman took a capsule, grinned at each other, then swallowed.

"It dissolves your fat. And leaves you looking—" Estelle held up a finger "—stick thin!"

"How does it work?" asked Patricia.

Estelle gave a high-pitched titter that could have shattered glass. The same way she'd laughed when they'd all called her fat as a "joke."

"Flesh-eating bacteria."

Spare the Rod

Taylor Crook

Father Townsend knew how to deal with difficult boys.

"You pulled away from the ruler, Peter." The paddle struck. "You can't shirk discipline."

"I was trying to save her. Sister Vera's not so bad. She doesn't enjoy it like you do."

"Enjoy what?"

"Hurting us. I can't control it when I'm hurt."

"Stop it, Peter. Spare the rod…"

The wooden paddle struck the child, and a dark form burst from Peter's back. His head turned, looking over his shoulder with black eyes. Shadowy tendrils wrapped Father Townsend in a grotesque embrace.

A booming voice emerged from the boy, "Spoil the child."

One Bad Step

Chris Jorgensen

Sometimes the worst part of a scary situation has none of the elements of the films I saw as a kid. I was always afraid of the slasher running around a neighborhood killing anyone in their path. I watched the news about serial killers snatching up people and taking them to their torture chambers. I read books of monsters and creatures in the night who want to do me harm for no other reason than I exist. Turns out, the real terror comes from simply falling down my basement stairs badly enough when I live alone.

No one will find me.

Vision

Jo Birdwell

Lisa was condescending to the hospital staff, demanding special attention due to her new "handicap." Whenever the nurses checked in on her, Lisa would continue her "blind" charade and scolded them for not being more considerate. The staff scoffed at the nurses' station, "She's got minor burns to the pupils. She'll be fine soon."

A night nurse found Lisa during one of her tirades and presented new "special" eye drops.

When the drops were administered, Lisa's eyes reddened, twitched, watered, and burned. Her vision slowly darkened until there was nothing left.

The last thing Lisa saw was the nurse's smiling face.

Playing Pretend

Brianna Malotke

Kate sighed as she pulled her car into her driveway. Even in the darkness, she noticed the cars of several friends parked on the streets nearby. She understood why her partner urged her to stop for chips.

She took a deep breath, calming her mind.

She headed to the front door, her hand hesitating on the knob. With time, Kate had learned how to fake her emotions, so she could pretend to be surprised. Besides, it wasn't her actual birthday, but that of the woman she murdered ten years ago.

Plastering a fake smile on her face, she opened the door.

It's Who You Know

Keyra Kristoffersen

Blinded by the snow glare, Jim stalled, head whipping back and forth. Searching. Only empty branches stared back at him, lifeless and cruel. His whole body stung with the cold, but escape was everything.

Crunch.

She stood, watching him, saying nothing.

"Please, honey, we don't have to do this," he begged, hands reaching out to the wife he barely recognized. "We can get away from them. They can't make us play their sick game. We can leave. Together."

Crimson splattered the snow before the echo of the gunshot ceased.

"Congratulations," said a loud, booming voice behind her. "We have a winner!"

Eyes in the Cracks

Elizabeth Suggs

In the darkest hours, eyes protrude from the cracks in my walls. Eyes that slink up between the boards, becoming mush as they slip out into my room. These eyes watch me, unblinking, even as I dim the lights and keep my tired lids open. But I hear their bits and pieces squish and slither, edging closer to me. I know if I go to sleep now, they'll snatch up my sight, just like they did to my mother. I should have been with her that night, watching. But I was sleeping.

They are coming, but I'm too fatigued to resist.

Senior Prank or Big Mistake?

AudraKate Gonzalez

"You're kidding, right?" Mila asked. She didn't believe me until I opened my bathroom door.

"You stole the cadaver from the lab?!" She stared at the body in shock.

"It's a senior prank! A good one at that." I looked down at the naked corpse in my bathtub. Mr. Javorsky, our professor, would lose his head over this tomorrow.

"What if the administration finds out and then they don't let you graduate?!" Mila's face went bright red.

"Mila, it's going to be fine. No one will find out. What could possibly go wrong?"

The hand on the corpse twitched in response.

Poor Lilly Didn't Listen

Brianna Malotke

Standing alone on the cracked sidewalk, Lilly stared at the cobblestone pathway leading up to the Wildridge Manor. She had heard the stories growing up, knew that evil lurked within those walls.

She took one step closer. The manor seemed to whisper her name. Lilly had heard all the warnings, and yet, she continued. Maybe the house was beckoning her. She just wanted to peek in the cracked windows. But the second her hand touched the doorknob, her body had to enter.

The door closed behind her.

No one ever saw Lilly again, the girl who dared enter the cursed home.

Hidden Beauty

McKenzie Richardson

"Bet you're real pretty under that mask," Nick cooed. "Why don't you take it off? Shame to hide such beauty."

The girl giggled behind the ivory mask painted with roses and vines, but she kept the covering in place.

"Come on, I'd love to see what's underneath." Nick reached for the mask, but the girl grabbed his wrist. "Just a tiny peek."

Never one to take no for an answer, Nick shook away her grip and pulled at the disguise.

A pair of glowing amber eyes stared at Nick.

The last thing he heard was hissing snakes reverberating in his ears.

Bullied

H. V. Patterson

Ren was walking home alone when CJ swaggered up to him.

"Why're you carrying a purse?"

"It's not a purse," Ren said.

"Did you get it from your dead mommy?" jeered CJ.

He grabbed the weathered messenger bag, and Ren let him take it.

"What do you have in here? Tampons?"

CJ shoved his hand inside. Nothing. He pushed his whole arm into the bag. Nothing but emptiness.

"What the hell—"

Something seized CJ's wrist and pulled. CJ screamed as he was slurped into the bag.

The bag burped and snapped shut.

"Told you it wasn't a purse," Ren muttered.

Hunting

Keyra Kristoffersen

Broken, searing, slicing agony.

Chad cracked his good eye open, the light smokey and orange. A fire blazed.

"Ah, there you are," growled a low voice in the haze, "It's no fun if you're asleep."

Paralyzed, aching, his calf caught in a steel bear trap, Chad whimpered. Fierce pain exploded as an unfamiliar person prodded his naked belly with a knife—a gut-hook. *His* gut-hook, the one packed on his hunts.

"So, you like to skin defenseless animals?" Sickly ichor flowed freely from the wound as the knife sliced open the skin of his navel. "Let's see how you like it."

In the Shadows

Debra Birdwell Winkler

The Tombstone Strangler was still at large, but that didn't deter me. I still visited Nana's grave every evening after work.

Darkness enclosed around as the cold wind whipped through the trees. The moon followed me through the graveyard, casting eerie shadows across the lawn.

I knelt and placed her favorite flowers, purple lilies, upon her grave.

As I said a prayer, rough hands enclosed around my throat. While I choked, I saw a flutter of white appear and fling the man against a mausoleum, bleeding.

"Not my granddaughter!" the spirit called.

"Nana?"

The wind settled, and the spirit was gone.

Turning a Blind Eye

Alison Chesley

Erich struggled against the straps on the operating table. The screams of the dead who came before him echoed in his mind's eye.

He gasped as a diminutive Doctor Muntel hovered over him with a large needle.

"The new solution will surely turn his eyes from brown to blue," the doctor said to his colleague and moved to inject Erich's iris.

Erich broke free from the restraints and shoved the doctor's arm out of the way, stabbing the needle in the doctor's eye. Within seconds, his eyes went a bright blue.

His screams could be heard down the hall, "I'm blind!"

Bonus Points

Jonathan Reddoch

Moans erupted from sullen faces gathered around the posted grades for the biochem final.

The mob turned to the source of their anguish: Billy Thorndyke at his lab station, meticulously squeezing green droplets into a purple beaker.

"You absolute nerd!"

"Ruined the curve!"

"101 out of 100!"

"He even got the bonus question!"

One boy grabbed Billy's backpack and turned on the burner.

Unperturbed, Billy glanced up at the amassing seniors through his fogging goggles. "What's the product when mixing diphosphorus-sulfates with tungsten-carbide in a biological specimen?"

They shrugged. Billy swallowed the contents; his eyes burned phosphorescent purple. "Time you learned."

Author Bios

Abby Bathurst

Abby Bathurst is a UK motorsport journalist and podcaster for FormulaNerds. She is also a blogger and owner of the site writewatchwork.com and a popular bookstagrammer on Instagram @WriteWatchWork. Writing for Abby is an escape and she's grateful to be able to share her words with others. When she's not writing, Abby is often reading, listening to music or spending time with family and friends.

Abby's story appears on page: 72

Addison Smith

Addison Smith has blood made of cold brew and flesh made of chocolate. He spends most of his time writing about fish, birds, and cybernetics, often in combination. His fiction has appeared in Fantasy Magazine, Fireside Magazine, *and* Daily Science Fiction, *among others.*

Addison's story appears on page: 1

Aiden E. Messer

Aiden was born and raised in Switzerland. They have always loved reading and writing, and have long had a fascination for the macabre. They had to put their interest in writing on hold for a few years, while they finished their studies. They now have a master's degree in psychology, and have been able to get back to writing on a much more regular basis.

Aiden's story appears on page: 56

Alex Child

Writing has a unique power, and Alex Child is just smart enough to know that he's nowhere near smart enough to accu-

rately describe it. Between working half as hard as he should and twice as hard as required at his day job, he continues pursuing that indescribable emotional swell from relating to a literary character and sharing their experiences. He hopes his stories brings you even just a portion of that rush. Alex has been published in Collective Darkness, Little Darkness, The Darkness Between, Collective Visions, Little Visions, Collective Fantasy, *and* Little Fantasy.

Alex's stories appear on pages: 6, 23, 47, 79

Alison Chesley

Alison Chesley is a licensed master esthetician whose lifelong love for the written word has inspired her to study communications and writing. She grew up in a large family in Bountiful, Utah, but lived many years on the west side of Oahu. She draws from her vivid imagination, dreams, and past trauma for inspiration.

Alison's story appears on page: 100

Anne Gregg

Anne Gregg is a college student, writer, and poet from Northwest Indiana. Her short stories have been published in the anthologies Kids Are Hell! *and* Collective Fantasy. *Her poetry has been featured in* Noctivagant Press, *and the* Black Poppy Review.

Anne's story appears on page: 69

Ashley Huyge

Ashley Huyge is a writer, educator, and course designer. A long-time lover of speculative fiction and horror, she finds dark and unexpected themes a comforting way to explore the things that scare us. She finds that reading and writing horror is the safest way to enjoy recreational fear. Her writing has appeared in Dreams Walking, *and she is currently editing a horror/speculative fiction novel. A transplant living in Southern California, she enjoys supernatural movies, Americanos, and sunshine from a shaded vantage point. She lives with her husband, her cats, and her dreams.*

Ashley's stories appear on pages: 10, 35, 66, 81

AudraKate Gonzalez

AudraKate Gonzalez started writing horror stories when she ran out of Goosebumps *books to read as a child. Her love for horror grew and now she has a BA in Creative Writing and is working on her MFA. Her YA/Horror Series,* This is

Noir, *is available now wherever you buy your books. She lives in Ohio with her handsome husband, and her adorable furry bad boys, Zero and Scrappy Doo. When AudraKate isn't writing, you can find her reading, watching scary movies or sleeping. You can learn more about AudraKate by following her on TikTok or Instagram @lets.get.lit.erature or visit her website www.authoraudrakategonzalez.com*
AudraKate's stories appear on pages: 17, 44, 61, 94

Austin Slade Perry
As a child, Austin was always told he had an overactive imagination. When he grew up, that imagination transformed into storytelling and his passion for writing. He has been published in Collective Darkness, Little Darkness, Darkness Between, *and* Collective Fantasy.
Austin's stories appear on pages: 5, 25, 36, 63

Brianna Malotke
Brianna Malotke is a writer and member of the Horror Writers Association based in the PNW. Her most recent work can be found in Dark Town, The Nottingham Horror Collective *and* HorrorScope: A Zodiac Anthology. *She also has horrifying poems and short stories in the anthologies* Beneath, Cosmos, The Deep, Beautiful Tragedies 2, The Dire Circle, Out of Time, Their Ghoulish Reputation, Holiday Leftovers, *and* Under Her Skin. *In August 2023, her debut horror poetry collection,* Fashion Trends, Deadly Ends, *will be released by Green Avenue Books. For more malotkewrites.com*
Brianna's stories appear on pages: 11, 32, 91, 95

Chris Jorgensen
Chris has often been described as an amalgamation of too many things for his own good. Writer, musician, academic, book collector, scavenger, builder, drinker, shiny object enthusiast. Horror is the gateway to the truly primal, the unknown void, and the creative outlet that can be explored without fear. He has written for online publications and short story collections for Utah Valley University. Currently, he reads far too much to have a singular favorite author, but is often inspired by: Patrick Rothfuss, Robert Jordan, H.P. Lovecraft, Stephen King, Brandon Sanderson, and Joe Abercrombie. One day he will be hopefully as well read as that list. Chris has also been published in Collective Darkness.
Chris' stories appear on pages: 4, 30, 58, 89

Conor Bennett
Conor Bennett is an electrical engineer and Coast Guard veteran with a passion for crafting chilling tales. Growing up immersed in the worlds of Goosebumps *and* Tales from the Crypt, *he developed a deep appreciation for the macabre and a love for all things horror. When he's not conjuring up haunting tales, Conor can be found immersed in the world of tabletop gaming, where he serves as a dungeon master for epic* Dungeons and Dragons *adventures. Conor is currently developing a children's horror anthology series with his wife, Jenifer.*
Conor's stories appear on pages: 9, 41, 62

Debra Birdwell Winkler
Debra Birdwell Winkler is a published author who is passionate about sharing her stories. As a former history teacher, Debra weaves historical events into her stories as well as music. Whether publishing short stories, novels, or poems, she excitedly devotes full concentration on writing—her focus, her job, and her joy (second only to her family). Her debut novel Cycle of Coincidence *was released in November 2022. Several of her short stories have been published in Anthologies, like her story "Never in a Million Years" in Second Chance, a nonprofit romance anthology, as well as others have been released online. In 2022, she was nominated for the 2022 Best of the Net NonFiction Award.*
Debra's story appears on page: 99

D. J. James
D. J. James grew up with a love of storytelling and has wanted to be a writer since he was a child. He attended Oakland University in Auburn Hills, Michigan and graduated with a BA in Graphic Design and a BA in Creative Writing. He self-published his debut novel, My Dark Fairy Tale, in 2021.
D.J.'s stories appear on pages: 64

Elizabeth Suggs
Elizabeth Suggs is the co-owner of the indie publisher Collective Tales Publishing, owner of Editing Mee, the founder of the LUW Romance Writers Chapter, and the author of a growing number of published stories, two of which were in a podcast and poetry journal. She is a book reviewer on EditingMee.com and popular bookstagramer and cosplayer on Instagram: @ElizabethSuggsAuthor. Elizabeth has been published in over a dozen

anthologies, including Collective Darkness, Little Darkness, The Darkness Between, Collective Visions, Little Visions, Collective Fantasy, Little Fantasy, *and featured in* Tales from the Monoverse. *When she's not writing or reading, she's playing video and board games or making cookies.*

Elizabeth's stories appear on pages: 2, 26, 38, 60, 86, 93

Ethan Reisler
Ethan Reisler, born and raised in Maryland, is majoring in English at Messiah University where he also works as the head editor-in-chief for the campus magazine, The Swinging Bridge. *Alongside writing and editing for the collegiate magazine, Ethan has also been published in* Horror From the High Dive: Volume 2 *for his short story "And the Days Lengthened." Although most of his time is spent working and studying, Ethan still makes time for reading, writing, playing video games and hanging out with his friends.*

Ethan's story appears on page: 27

F. Malanoche
F. Malanoche writes under the cover of night, hoping to bring authentic and odd Latino stories into the world. He teaches English in the Midwest, has a wonderful wife, and sweet vinyl collection. You can follow him on his Facebook page F. Malanoche.

F. Malanoche's story appears on page: 67

Gully Novaro
Gully's stories appear on pages: 45, 70

H. V. Patterson
H. V. Patterson lives in Oklahoma and writes speculative fiction and poetry. She's a cofounder of Horns and Rattles Press and runs Dreadfulesque. She has stories and poems published or upcoming with Sliced Up Press, Creature Publishing, Flame Tree Press, Eerie River, Flash Fiction Online, and Black Spot Books. When she isn't reading and writing, she likes to hike and bake. Find her on Twitter @ScaryShelley and on Instagram @hvpattersonwriter

H. V.'s stories appear on pages: 24, 54, 97

Jenifer Schwendiman
Jenifer Schwendiman has a passion for storytelling in any format. She grew up immersed in the captivating worlds provided by books, movies, video games, and her own imagination; she believes stories are the most powerful way to explore and understand yourself and others. Drawing inspiration from the fears and shadows that lurk within us all, she is passionate about writing stories that delve into themes of dissociation, obsession, and the fragility of sanity. In her free time, Jenifer enjoys spending time with her husband, Conor, and her five feline friends, Brat, Duck, PopTart, Haunter, and Haru, who remind her daily of the beauty in imperfection and unconditional love. She can be found on Instagram and Twitch as @Jeniferbeast.
Jenifer's story appears on page: 52

Jo Birdwell
Jo Birdwell is a writer and full-time nurse from Texas who hopes to one day switch to writing full time. In the process of getting her bachelors degree in English and creative writing, she is an avid reader and writer with a strong passion for all things horror. Her short story "The Mortician's Daughter" was published in CTP's 2021 anthology Darkness Deluxe. *Her piece "Unlovable" was published in* Open Minds Quarterly's *spring 2022 issue.*
Jo's stories appear on pages: 21, 50, 90

Jonathan Reddoch
Jonathan Reddoch is co-owner of Collective Tales Publishing. He is a father, writer, editor, and publisher. He writes sci-fi, fantasy, romance, and especially horror. He has been working on his enormous sci-fi novel for over a decade and would like to finish it in this lifetime if possible. Find him on Instagram: @Allusions_of_Grandeur_ Jonathan has been published in a myriad of things, including Collective Darkness, Little Darkness, The Darkness Between, Collective Visions, Little Visions, Collective Fantasy, *and* Little Fantasy.
Jonathan's stories appear on pages: 3, 22, 39, 71, 78, 101

Joshua G. J. Insole
Three-time Reedsy winner Joshua G. J. Insole is a British writer who lives in the Austrian Alps. Author of several other

shortlisted stories, he published his first book in 2020. Joshua's favoured genres are horror and science fiction.

Joshua's stories appear on pages: 29, 77, 87

Katie Collupy
Katie Collupy is an epic grimdark fantasy author who delights in telling dark stories that explore the human condition. She is currently working on an epic fantasy multiverse dubbed the Dra-koverse, *and it starts with her debut fantasy novel,* Heir of Fates. *She is also published in* Collective Visions: Lost in Transmission *anthology. She has a bachelor's degree in criminal justice but spends her days writing and crafting fantastical worlds. When not writing she lives out her cottage core dreams in Vermont with her husband and three cats, Timbre, Wyndle, and Aragorn.*

Katie's story appears on page: 34

Kelly Mintzer
Kelly Mintzer is pleased as punch and absurdly honored to be featured in Darkness 101. She is a freelance writer with bylines spread, willy-nilly, across the internet. She is the author of Like I Used To, *a feminist slasher novel, and is featured in the collection* Tales from the Monoverse.

Kelly's story appears on page: 14

Keyra Kristoffersen
Keyra Kristoffersen is a born and bred reader who has no home, save it be the disgruntled arms of their gingers, Richard and Eustace. They've written a few short stories for magazines and online sources and worked as a Utah journalist for several years. The dream is to travel the world, play with animals, and write about it. They might even let their husband come along.

Keyra's stories appear on pages: 92, 98

K. R. Patterson
K. R. has been drawn to the dark side since she was a child. She knows that vampires are real, as are ghosts, demons, were-wolves, and serial killers. In fact, she has been compelled— probably by a vampire—into studying serial killers for fun. She often watches scary movies alone in a dark house with the curtains open. Other than contributing to this anthology, she's also been published in the Collective Darkness, Little Darkness, Deluxe Darkness, *and* Darkness Between *anthologies. She has a pirate novel out (available on Amazon and Audible), which is titled* A Dead Man's Tale. *She's been published in* Writer's

Digest *and has won various writing contests when she talked vampires into compelling the judges. She is currently getting her MFA in creative writing and working on her next novel about a cursed town.*
K. R.'s stories appear on pages: 7, 40, 68

Kristy Lytle
Kristy Lytle grew up in Alabama but now resides in Georgia with her husband and their two sons. When not writing, she enjoys reading horror novels, playing tennis, sweating her ass off in hot yoga, and dancing to hard rock and metal music. Kristy is a wine enthusiast (meaning she will enthusiastically drink wine) and loves going to the beach whenever possible.
Kristy's stories appear on pages: 18, 53

Margaret Gaffney
Margaret Gaffney is a new adult fantasy author specializing in plot driven stories, admirable heroes, and closed-door romance. Her published works include her All the Queen's Men series.
Margaret's story appears on page: 74

Megan Kiekel Anderson
Megan Kiekel Anderson (she/they) is a nerdy queer neurodivergent dark fiction writer. Her work can be found or is upcoming in such places as Flame Tree Press, Medusa Publishing Haus, Nightmare, and Monstrous Books. They live in Kansas City with their chaotic family including too many cats, chickens, and foster kittens. You can find her on Twitter and Instagram under the handle @megan_nerdnest or at her website at www. megankiekelanderson.com.
Megan's story appears on pages: 12

McKenzie Richardson
McKenzie Richardson lives in Milwaukee, WI. A lifelong explorer of the dark corners of imagined worlds, she's spent the past few years chronicling her findings. Her work can be found in publications from Iron Faerie Publishing, Eerie River Publishing, Black Ink Fiction, and Nordic Press. McKenzie currently works as a librarian, doing her best not to be buried beneath an ever-growing TBR list. When not writing, she can usually be found in her book hoard, armed with coffee and a good book.
McKenzie's stories appear on pages: 33, 73, 83, 96

Morgana Price
Morgana Price loves the spooky and the beautiful. She often takes her dark and freaky dreams and turns them into stories—much like her entries in this anthology. As the alter ego of author Alicia Morley Dodson, Price's name was inspired by Morgana of Arthurian legends and the surname of Price from the late and great Vincent Price—whose laugh at the end of Michael Jackson's "Thriller" gives her goosebumps. This is Price's first publication @morganapriceofficial. She fantasizes being a gothic goddess adorned in red and black gowns with rubies, black opal, and onyx. When she's not writing, she's watching movies, enjoying amateur flora photography, and baking cupcakes.
Morgana's stories appear on pages: 57, 80

Natalya Monyok
Natalya Monyok is an avid lover of all things horror, choosing to get lost within the madness instead of succumbing to the mundanities of the mortal world. She is currently seeking representation for her psychological horror novel, Mortal Minds. *When she's not putting her characters into terrible situations, she's been known to train Brazilian Jiu Jitsu relentlessly. She is a blue belt in the martial art and hopes to achieve her black belt and open up her own academy one day. She lives in the suburbs of Utah with her loyal dog Ares, close to both Salt Lake City and the beautiful mountains.*
Natalya's stories appear on pages: 8, 59

Nicholas Yanes
Nicholas Yanes, Ph.D. has over a decade of experience researching and writing about entertainment industries as an academic, journalist, and corporate consultant. His research expertise is on the evolution of entertainment businesses and specializes in the spaces of gaming, transmedia, tech adoption, and IP development.
Nicholas' stories appear on pages: 16, 76

Nina Tolstoy
Nina is a writer, storyteller, playwright and immersive theatre creator. Much of Nina's current creative practice involves interactive, immersive, and experiential theatre. She writes independently, as well as for Electric Goldfish *(digital and in-person immersive theatre) and* Incognito Experiences *(be-*

spoke theatrical adventures and alternate reality games). She has had short plays produced in London and NYC, and was a contributor to Hotel Wonderland *in 2022, the Netherlands largest immersive theatre production. Nina has had short fiction published online, and recently in* Horrorscope Volume 1—*an anthology of dark fiction. She is currently writing her first work of ergodic fiction.*

Nina's stories appear on pages: 28, 49, 84

Paul Lonardo
Paul Lonardo is a freelance writer and author with numerous titles of both fiction and nonfiction books. He's placed dark fiction and nonfiction articles in various genre magazines and ezines. Most recently, his collection of 365 haiku horror poems, titled Penny Dreadfuls, *was published this past summer, and* Small Dark Things, *an anthology of new dark fantasy and horror stories, will be released in October 2023. He is a contributing writer for* Tales from the Moonlit Path *and an active HWA member. A longtime baseball fan, when not writing, Paul helps coach his teenage son's travel baseball team.*

Paul's stories appear on pages: 46, 65

Peter Hayward-Bailey
Peter Hayward-Bailey is a husband, father and lifelong horror lover, ever since seeing Gremlins *at a young age and being utterly terrified by it. Peter created the instagram page and blog "Positively Horror" in early 2020 to share his love of the genre and combat negativity in the online horror community. From there, he has had the opportunity to interview many great names in horror, which led to becoming a staff writer and short horror editor for* Morbidly Beautiful. *After spending some time writing articles and reviews, Peter wanted to turn his creative energy to fiction, and has been writing short stories for the last couple of years. As well as all this, Peter plays lead guitar in UK glam metallers Bad Behaviour.*

Peter's stories appear on pages: 43, 85

Peter L. Harmon
Peter L. Harmon is a Maryland based TV producer, screenwriter, podcaster, and author. He is the writer of The Happenstances... young adult book series, the editor of the Horror From The High Dive *horror anthologies for High Dive Publishing, and he has contributed short stories to a handful of other anthologies.*

Peter was featured in The Baltimore Sun's 2022 article "Season's Readings: 10 Books From Baltimore-Area Authors To Add to Your Holiday Wish List." You can see what he's up to by following @HighDivePublishing on Instagram, and you can listen to his podcast The VamPetey Diaries, *a* The Vampire Diaries *rewatch podcast, on any of the major podcast platforms.*

Peter's stories appear on pages: 13, 37, 75

Peter V. Hilton
Peter lives with his longsuffering spouse and rambunctious young family in the Cincinnati metro area, where writing provides an enjoyable (and sometimes necessary!) reprieve from his professional career. Although working as a business lawyer finds him crunching numbers as often as crafting words, ages past have seen him published in print periodicals and as a digital marketing writer, and he is a onetime prizewinning poet. More recently he published the fantasy epic A King for Ravens, *his first novel, which is the beginning of an anticipated trilogy.*

Peter's stories appear on pages: 55

P. S. Tom
P. S. Tom makes his debut published short story with Collective Tales Publishing. He is a husband, father, writer and entrepreneur. When not writing, he can be found in the shadows building Halloween attractions for theme parks, musicians or movie studios. He is a real estate investor and broker. He is currently working on a horror and mystery short story series. Find him on Instagram: @p.s.tom_author

P. S.'s story appears on page: 31

Robin Knabel
Robin Knabel's short fiction has appeared in The Raven Review, Hope Screams Eternal, Autumn Noir, Summer Bludgeon, *and* Still of Winter. *She has also placed in the Writer's Digest Your Story Contest and the NYC Midnight Short Story & Microfiction Challenges. Robin is currently working on publishing a personal collection of horror short stories through her Inky Bones Press label and enjoys sharing book reviews and photography on robinknabel.com. Robin is a co-owner of Unsettling Reads.*

Robin's stories appear on pages: 19, 48, 82

Taylor Crook
Taylor Crook is a fantasy author living in Hamilton, Ontario with his beautiful wife and two German Shepherds. Before taking on a writing career his life was shaped by nearly two decades in the restaurant industry. Long nights in bustling dining rooms have proven to be an invaluable and beloved step on a journey that led to finally achieving the dream of being a published author. When he's not writing, Taylor enjoys basketball, drumming, video games and, the hobby that started it all, reading. His favourite activity, though, is anything that he gets to do with his wife.
Taylor's stories appear on pages: 20, 51, 88

Teasha Lynn
Teasha Lynn is new to the writing world. This will be her first publication since childhood. She has had a great passion for literature. Now, she is taking a risk to find a career within her life-long love. When she is not building her skill as an author, she finds joy in video games and the outdoors. She grew up in an extremely close-knit family. Teasha is dedicating her first published work to her two little sisters: Ceysha Maree, and Alee Ahn. It is through their unconditional love that Teasha found the courage to chase her dreams.
Teasha's story appears on page: 15

Thomas S. Salem
Thomas S. Salem has a bachelor's in english literature. He is an avid reader of fiction. He has been telling stories since he was a child. Within the last two years he finally got the courage to share his work with an audience that went beyond immediate family and friends.
Thomas' story appears on page: 42

Check Out Our Other Anthologies:

Collective Darkness: A Horror Anthology

Deluxe Darkness: Three Books in One

Collective Fantasy: An Unsavory Anthology

Collective Visions: Lost in Transmission

Collective Chaos: An Apocalyptic Anthology (Coming Soon!)

Collective Humanity: An LGBTQ+ Anthology (Coming Soon!)

Collective Madness: Schisms of the Soul (Coming Soon!)

www.CTPFiction.com

Are You a Writer?

Submit to one of our upcoming anthologies!

Collective Chaos: An Apocalyptic Anthology

Collective Humanity: An LGBTQ+ Anthology

Collective Madness: Schisms of the Soul

Darkness 102: Advanced Lessons Were Learned

www.CTPFiction.com

Printed in the USA
CPSIA information can be obtained
at www.ICGtesting.com
LVHW030157160923
758334LV00018B/342